THE MANY COLORS OF HARPREET SINGH

BY
SUPRIYA KELKAR

iLLUSTRATED BY
ALEA MARLEY

STERLING CHILDREN'S BOOKS
New York

And he wore **white** when he felt shy,
not wanting to be seen.

"Do you want to wear red?"
his mom asked.

"No reason to be brave,"
Harpreet replied.

"How about pink?"
asked his dad.

"What's there to celebrate?"
said Harpreet.

"Maybe all you need . . ." said his
mom, "is a little sunshine!"

Harpreet shook his head and sighed. "Look outside. No birds. No blooms. No beach. Just cold."

For Leykh, Zuey, and Arjun —S.K.

For Zoe and Patrick —A.M.

STERLING CHILDREN'S BOOKS
New York

An Imprint of Sterling Publishing Co., Inc.
1166 Avenue of the Americas
New York, NY 10036

STERLING and the distinctive Sterling logo are
registered trademarks of Sterling Publishing Co., Inc.

Text © 2019 Supriya Kelkar
Cover and interior illustrations © 2019 Alea Marley
Afterword © 2019 Simran Jeet Singh

ISBN 978-1-4549-3184-3

Distributed in Canada by Sterling Publishing Co., Inc.
c/o Canadian Manda Group, 664 Annette Street
Toronto, Ontario M6S 2C8, Canada
Distributed in the United Kingdom by GMC Distribution Services
Castle Place, 166 High Street, Lewes, East Sussex BN7 1XU, England
Distributed in Australia by NewSouth Books
University of New South Wales, Sydney, NSW 2052, Australia

For information about custom editions, special sales,
and premium and corporate purchases,
please contact Sterling Special Sales at 800-805-5489
or specialsales@sterlingpublishing.com.

Manufactured in China

Lot #
2 4 6 8 10 9 7 5 3 1
06/19

sterlingpublishing.com

Interior and cover design by Heather Kelly
The artwork in this book was created digitally.